# The Tribes of Redwall
## Mice

## BRIAN JACQUES

# Tales of Redwall

- Lord Brocktree
- Martin the Warrior
- Mossflower
- The Legend of Luke
- Outcast of Redwall
- Mariel of Redwall
- The Bellmaker
- Salamandastron
- Redwall
- Mattimeo
- The Pearls of Lutra
- The Long Patrol
- Marlfox
- The Taggerung
- The Tribes of Redwall: Badgers
- The Tribes of Redwall: Otters

THE TRIBES OF REDWALL: MICE
A RED FOX BOOK 0 09 941414 7
Published in Great Britain by Red Fox,
an imprint of Random House Children's Books
This edition published 2003. 1 3 5 7 9 10 8 6 4 2
Introduction copyright © The Redwall Abbey Company Ltd, 2003
Text copyright © Random House Children's Books, 2003
Illustrations copyright © Jonathan Walker, 2003
The right of Brian Jacques and Jonathan Walker
to be identified as the author and illustrator of this work
has been asserted in accordance with the Copyright, Designs and Patents Act 1988.
All rights reserved.
Red Fox Books are published by Random House Children's Books,
61–63 Uxbridge Road, London W5 5SA,
a division of The Random House Group Ltd,
in Australia by Random House Australia (Pty) Ltd,
20 Alfred Street, Milsons Point, Sydney, NSW 2061, Australia,
in New Zealand by Random House New Zealand Ltd,
18 Poland Road, Glenfield, Auckland 10, New Zealand,
and in South Africa by Random House (Pty) Ltd,
Endulini, 5A Jubilee Road, Parktown 2193, South Africa
THE RANDOM HOUSE GROUP Limited Reg. No. 954009
www.kidsatrandomhouse.co.uk
Printed in Hong Kong
A CIP catalogue record for this book is available from the British Library.

# The Tribes of Redwall
# Mice

## INTRODUCTION

*I*t is a simple truth: without mice, there would be no Redwall. Only a tribe that can embrace, at one and the same time, such widely different characters as a great warrior and an outrageous, irrepressible Prince of Mousethieves could so successfully weld together a community of goodbeasts bound by friendship, loyalty and honour – ties that strengthen, but never restrict. Vermin chieftains, on the other hand, use far baser methods, controlling their hordes through fear, or envy, or greed – until somebeast stronger comes along. And, when you owe your position to brute strength alone, there is always somebeast stronger.

Remember, too, that even the mightiest weapon is only as strong as the beast who wields it – and that the sword of Martin the Warrior, which destroyed so much evil and cleared the way for so much good, could as easily have wreaked havoc and destruction in the wrong paws. That is why Luke tells Martin he must only raise it in a good cause: because possession of a blade capable of both good and evil carries with it a great responsibility.

So here they are, the mice of Redwall, in all their diversity: gentle Columbine, the perfect mate for a mousethief; keen fighter Mariel, the most resilient of mousemaids; practical Cornflower, calmly organizing the defence of the abbey while her heart is on the plains with Matthias and Mattimeo; and, sword in the one's paw and a reed flute in the other's, that pair of giants: Martin and Gonff.

Redwall for everrrrrrr!

*Brian Jacques*

# The Mouse Tribe ❖—

While all woodlanders of goodwill are welcome in Redwall, the heart of the abbey remains its ancient order of mouse brothers and sisters, who from the time of its founder Abbess Germaine have been dedicated to the service of their fellow creatures.

## THE ORDER

It is said that when Martin forsakes the way of the warrior and lays aside his sword, the order he helps to establish at Redwall Abbey finds its true vocation. All the mice take a solemn vow never to harm another living creature, except in defence of the good. They promise to heal the sick, care for the injured and give aid to the wretched and impoverished. Their food they take from the earth, in return caring for the land and living in harmony with the seasons. Above all, they heal and protect their friends and brethren, only raising paw to do battle when their very way of life is threatened.

## THE ABBEY

Although it is Abbess Germaine who draws up the plans for a fine abbey complex to be constructed of local sandstone, and to incorporate orchards, fields and a fish pond, her dream only becomes reality with the help of Martin the Warrior, her co-founder. And there is more to the great red-walled building which presently rises amid the surrounding woodland than meets the eye, for both Martin and Germaine are gifted with a foresight that leads them to include in the structure all sorts of secrets to be interpreted by future generations: the riddle Martin leaves for Matthias, for instance, and Abbess Germaine's message for the time when Mattimeo will be stolen by a slaving party. As Abbot Mordalfus says on that occasion: 'Everything our ancestors built into Redwall has a story or a reason.'

## HEALERS AND HERBALISTS

From the beginning, the order of Redwall maintains the tradition of healing established by the brothers and sisters of Loamhedge. Skilled herbalists like blind Simeon, Columbine and Abbess Germaine herself hone their knowledge until the abbey infirmary is famed – some might say notorious – for its 'physicking'. Sister Cicely's warm nettle broth is feared by all, while there are those who do not hesitate to dub Sister Alkanet a poisoner. But at times of crisis, like the occasion of Martin's near-fatal wounding at the paws of Tsarmina, or the epidemic of Dryditch fever which seems set to decimate the Redwallers, the understanding of plants and their properties is invaluable. In the kitchens, too, it has its uses, as the most delicious flavours are created from root and berry, flower and leaf.

## SCHOLARS AND SCHEMERS

According to Brother Hoben, the Recorder's job is 'to shed the light of knowledge and learning by keeping our abbey's records', and given their turn for scholarship, mice like Barlom and Hubert, Hoben and Hal fit very naturally into the post. As youngsters they are excellent scholars: it is John Churchmouse who remembers enough of his lessons to translate some ancient Loamscript in time to save Mattimeo. Quick wits are helpful in more devious ways, too, as Sister May demonstrates when she immobilizes the huge red kite Stryke in order to mend her broken wing. Cornflower dreams up the ghost plan to subdue the raven General Ironbeak and his cohorts; and Sister Withe's expertise is crucial in the plot to catch ferretbabe Veil red-handed.

## MISCHIEVOUS MOUSEBABES

'Like father, like son,' they say of Gonflet, pride and joy of
Columbine and the Prince of Mousethieves;
and expressions like 'a young pickle', 'a
right pair of little scallywags' and 'a
rogue and a scamp, the worst of all the
Dibbuns' are bandied about pretty freely
by the elders when the subjects under
discussion are Dandin, the Churchmouse
twins or the Mousebabe of Joseph the
Bellmaker's day. Somehow it always seems

to be a young mouse who falls off the abbey wall, like
Feegle, or into the excavations, like Sloey – although those
who know Sloey in later seasons would never have
recognized that mischievous creature in their sedate
Infirmary Sister. And as for Dwopple, the terror of the
Wandering Noonvale Companions . . .

## MIGHTY WARRIORS

Ever since the first Martin cleared the way for the
construction of Redwall Abbey in Mossflower Wood, a
warrior has emerged in times of trouble to defend the
abbeydwellers and defeat their enemies – and every one has
carried the Champion's great sword. First to lift the mighty
weapon in the service of his fellows is Dandin, who is also
the one who causes it to be laid in its intended hiding place
when the danger is over. Seasons later comes Matthias,
whose baby son Mattimeo knows almost from birth that the
one thing he wants in life is to wield that mesmerizing
blade. Mattimeo's son Martin succeeds him as Abbey
Warrior, and proves himself worthy of his name. The role of
Abbey Champion does not always fall to a mouse –
squirrels too can be excellent warriors, and an otter also
holds the honour – but the mice are among the bravest and
the best.

## THE JOSEPH BELL

The great bell that is the pride of Redwall until the time of
Matthias has a strange history. Originally commissioned for
his mountain stronghold by the Badger Lord, Rawnblade
Widestripe, it is destined never to reach
Salamandastron. On the voyage north
it is stolen by searats and taken to
Terramort, to be gloated over in
private by Rawnblade's arch-
enemy Gabool the Wild until
the bellmaker, his daughter and
Lord Rawnblade himself join
forces on the island to
destroy the Searat King.
Then, in gratitude to
Martin the Warrior,
whose spirit has saved
his life, Lord Rawnblade
resolves to give the bell to Redwall – an outcome predicted
by the ancient badger symbols round its top, together with
its name, Joseph, after its creator.

## MATTHIAS AND METHUSELAH

And so the Joseph Bell rings out for weddings, warnings
and celebrations, until the coming of Cluny the Scourge.
The big rat and his vermin horde gain access to Redwall
through blackmail and treachery, but by then Matthias has
found the sword of Martin the Warrior, and he wields it
skilfully. The end comes when he uses it to sever the rope
which holds the Joseph Bell to its stout timber axle, and
the bell drops like a stone right on top of Cluny. The
impact cracks it clear through the centre, and the two
pieces are recast into a pair of smaller bells, which the
Redwallers call Matthias and Methuselah, after the mouse
who saves them and the one who is his mentor.

## A SPECIAL SWORD

Luke the Warrior speaks words that predict the future
when he hands his sword to young Martin on the
northland shore. 'Always use the sword to stand for good
and right . . . and never let another creature take this
sword from you, not as long as you live.' Even after the
blade is snapped by Tsarmina the wildcat, Martin is never
seen without the hilt hanging from a cord around his neck.
And it is thus that he travels to Salamandastron in search
of the Badger Lord, Boar the Fighter, when Mossflower
seems likely to fall for ever beneath Tsarmina's paw. In
fulfilment of an ancient prophecy, Boar fashions a new
blade for the sword out of metal from a falling star and
forges it to the venerable hilt, which he re-straps with
hard black leather and finishes with a red pommel
stone. The fascinating weapon in paw, Martin returns
to Mossflower a true warrior.

After Martin's death, the sword remains
at Redwall, hidden, as Luke has instructed,
where only a true warrior would dare go to
find it. Martin himself selects its hiding
place, along an arm of the weather vane
atop the abbey's highest tower. But as is
the way of warriors he is buried with it
at his side, foreseeing that it will be
delivered to its destined place long
before the coming of Matthias,
in whom his own spirit will
live again.

## A TIME-HONOURED TAPESTRY

His great sword is not the only thing Martin inherits from
his father. Many seasons after Luke's death, Martin recovers
a beaded linen bag containing a woven portrait of Luke's
own father, another Martin. When he brings it back to
Mossflower, it is clear to all who see it that the spirit of

warriors and champions which shone from that older
Martin lives on in his son and grandson. So that when the
portrait is used as the centrepiece of a larger tapestry it
stands as a true portrayal of the founder of Redwall
himself, and is revered as such by all who come after him.

The Warrior is shown in full armour, leaning on the hilt
of his mighty sword, a smile on his face and his eyes
following anybeast looking for comfort or inspiration.
Those who worked the tapestry depicted vermin fleeing
from him in all directions, and below him, along the
tasselled bottom border, is embroidered the single word
'Martin'.

The tapestry comes to symbolize all the honour and
strength of Redwall, and word of it spreads throughout
Mossflower, reaching the ears of friend and foe alike.
Some of the latter covet it for its beauty, others because
they believe possession of it will deliver the abbey itself
into their paws, but whatever enemy steals it, it is never
long absent from its rightful place: the Great Hall of
Redwall Abbey.

# ❖ Mouse Habitat ❖

Not every Mossflower mouse is a member of the order
of Redwall. There are still those who, like their
predecessors in the time before the abbey is built, reap
crops in abundance or wring their subsistence from a
harsher land . . .

## OUTSIDE THE ORDER

At first the mouse tribes avoid the woodlands of
Mossflower, where owls and wildcats make their homes.
They favour the fertile middle lands, but not all are lucky
enough to find a haven like Noonvale, where the patriarch
Urran Voh invites all goodbeasts to thrive undisturbed in
peace and plenty. All too often the settlers are the target of
verminous villains who prey upon any who seek the
tranquil life, and must move on, searching for a place where
they do not have to sleep with one eye open. Thus the tribe
of Luke the Warrior come to the northland shore, where it
seems the good soil on the cliff-tops could be made to yield
sufficient crops for their needs, while they live securely in
the caves beneath . . .

## LOAMHEDGE

On the distant reaches of the plateau lands far to the south
of Mossflower, a peaceful community of mice dedicated to a
life of service live under the benevolent rule of their abbess,
Germaine. Like the Badger Lords of Salmandastron, they
have their own written language, Loamscript, and like the
Badger Lords they use their ancient symbols prophetically.
Matthias the Warrior is guided by just such a riddle to the
site of the old abbey, once a building nearly as large as
Redwall, now largely a subterranean ruin, since a long-ago
earthquake caused it to drop straight down into its own
cellars. Evil lodged in that underground complex, and
Matthias's conquest of that evil completes the destruction
of Loamhedge, with only some parts of the abbey remaining
above ground, hidden by seasons of growth.

## REDWALL

'A place o' safety an' cheer for goodbeasts to live in, with walls that'd stand the worst any vermin foes could think of!' That is Redwall Abbey, with its battlemented perimeter wall supporting a broad walkway, and its Great Hall, Cavern Hole, dormitories, kitchens, infirmary and bell tower. From the beginning it is conceived as a home for all woodlanders who wish to live in peace. And for that reason – besides the plentiful supply of local red sandstone – the chosen site is easily accessible on the east side of the path that runs from north to south through Mossflower Woods. The site, in fact, sits alongside an area once occupied by a distinctly different stronghold, Castle Kotir. This haunt of the wildcats who once terrorized the woodlanders is drowned under the lake created by the diversion of the River Moss, but over the seasons the lake begins to dry up, until by the time the abbey is well on the way to completion its existence has been all but forgotten. Thus it comes about that Redwall's south wall is built right over Kotir's north-west walltower – a fact which causes problems in the time of Abbess Tansy. But an army of mice, moles, squirrels, otters, hedgehogs and voles works with a will to repair the damage, and the abbey door is always open to all who are honest and of good heart, no matter what the season.

# Mouse Heroes

It is no accident that, like its first abbess, Redwall's first, and greatest, hero is a mouse. Mice combine spiritual strength with physical courage; mouse warriors and champions triumph over their enemies by the sheer power of their will and skill.

## ROSE

Appears in: *Martin the Warrior*

Martin calls her 'the warrior who uses the voice instead of the sword', and after her death it is said the beautiful, gentle creature with the wonderful singing voice is locked in Martin's heart, and there she is bound to stay. She saves his life when he would have been torn apart by sea birds, rescues him from the clutches of Badrang and leads him to the tranquil home of her tribe so that he can recruit followers to defeat the tyrant stoat. Yet, though Martin slays Badrang and wins back his father's sword, he loses something even more precious in that battle, to which he marches with an army at his back and Rose of Noonvale at his side.

## TIMBALLISTO

Appears in: *Mossflower, The Legend of Luke*

Three seasons older than his friend Martin, Timballisto is left in charge when Luke the Warrior sails from the northland shores. He defends the little colony valiantly, but the corsair raids are relentless and one day, inevitably, he is captured. Seasons later, Martin commandeers the searat Ripfang's ship and frees the galley slaves, including, to the Warrior's amazement and delight, his old comrade, Timballisto. Although their shared past is too painful to dwell on, their friendship endures and grows, and the tough older mouse proves a doughty ally in the great war of Mossflower, initiating the woodland creatures into the mysteries of the great siege catapults, or ballistae, which echo his name. He dies the following winter, and is mourned by all who knew him.

## GONFF THE MOUSETHIEF

Appears in: *Mossflower, The Legend of Luke*

Balladeer and flute-player, mischief-maker and mimic, the irrepressible Prince of Mousethieves makes friends wherever he goes. Orphaned as a babe, he is raised by kind Ben and Goodwife Stickle, and subsequently lives on his wits, his wisdom and his skill as a lockpick. He meets Martin the Warrior in the cells of Kotir, escapes with him to join the Council of

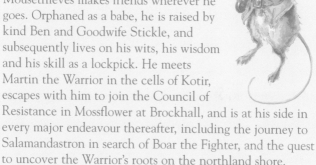

Resistance in Mossflower at Brockhall, and is at his side in every major endeavour thereafter, including the journey to Salamandastron in search of Boar the Fighter, and the quest to uncover the Warrior's roots on the northland shore. Happily mated with the lovely Columbine, he lives at Saint Ninian's – the very home from which Martin's father had been driven by Verdauga Greeneyes.

## COLUMBINE

Appears in: *Mossflower, The Legend of Luke*

One of the few survivors who accompanied Abbess Germaine from plague-stricken Loamhedge to join forces with Bella of Brockhall, the pretty young fieldmouse falls instantly under the spell of Gonff the Mousethief. The attraction is mutual, and by the time Gonff leaves with Martin to find Bella's father such a good understanding flourishes between them that their future together is taken for granted by all their friends. While Gonff is away, Columbine plans the destruction of Kotir with Foremole and Old Dinny, is taught to use a bow by the squirrelqueen Amber, and learns the gentler arts of healing and herblore from her mentor Abbess Germaine. To this day she is remembered with Gonff, Germaine and Martin himself as one of the great ones of Redwall Abbey.

## ABBESS GERMAINE
Appears in: *Mossflower, The Legend of Luke*

Mother Abbess of a peaceful order of builders and healers, Germaine is forced to leave her beloved Loamhedge when sickness strikes and seek shelter with her old friend Bella of Brockhall. She dreams of a time when Mossflower will be free of tyranny and she can found another community. And all through the turbulent days which culminate in Tsarmina's defeat she is drawing up plans for a great abbey where all good creatures can live in harmony with nature and each other. Having saved Martin's life after his last fight with the wildcat, she welcomes his help towards the realization of her dream; then, as first Abbess of Redwall, she sends him away to realize his own: to discover what happened to his father, Luke the Warrior.

## BRYONY
Appears in: *Outcast of Redwall*

Tough as a deep-rooted weed – that is the ferretbabe given into the charge of Bryony, the pretty great-granddaughter of Gonff the Mousethief who helps Friar Bunfold in the kitchens of Redwall Abbey. Bryony accepts the responsibility with delight, defending her protégé against unprovable accusations and apologizing for him when his guilt is undeniable. When he is banished from the abbey she follows him, saying simply, 'Because I'm responsible for him . . . I cannot desert him.' It is a painful learning process, but in the end she understands that inborn evil is irreclaimable – a sign of maturity acknowledged by Abbess Meriam when she names Bryony as her successor. As she says, Bryony's courage and compassion have never been in doubt, but her experience with Veil has added wisdom.

## JOSEPH THE BELLMAKER

Appears in: *Mariel of Redwall*,
*The Bellmaker*

He hails from the deep south: a strong,
sturdy mouse skilled in the casting of
metals, who gives his daughter a name
which rings out like the sound of a bell.
Separated from her when they are
captured at sea by Gabool the Wild,
Joseph escapes up the coast and slowly
builds up an army to overthrow the searat.
His joy when Mariel arrives can only be

imagined. Father and daughter fight together then, just as
they do seasons later when, guided by the spirit of Martin
the Warrior, Joseph leaves Redwall Abbey and travels to
Southsward to join the uprising against the usurper Urgan
Nagru. Joseph does not return from that land, electing to
stay to help rebuild the ravaged kingdom, but he never
forgets his friends in Mossflower.

## MARIEL

Appears in: *Mariel of Redwall*,
*The Bellmaker*

The little mousemaid can remember
nothing of the time before she is
washed up on the shore, battered by the
storm, with a knotted rope around her neck.
That rope proves a handy weapon against
marauding sea birds, and so it is as Storm
Gullwhacker that the mousemaid comes to
Mossflower. She left as Mariel, daughter of Joseph, who was
flung into the sea with a rock tied round her neck and only
survived because the rock was smashed to pieces against
another in the fall. A true warrior, she can never settle into
the peaceful, ordered life of Redwall Abbey, but must always
be off adventuring with her faithful companion Dandin –
returning, certainly, to spend seasons with her friends at
Redwall, but ever a wanderer at heart.

## METHUSELAH

Appears in: *Redwall*

'I like to think of myself as an aged but extremely erudite scholar,' says the ancient gatekeeper of Redwall – by far the oldest and wisest mouse in Mossflower. It is Methuselah who first suspects that Martin the Warrior lives again in Matthias; Methuselah who deciphers the coded directions to find the tomb and then the hiding place of the sword of the abbey's first Champion. His knowledge of the abbey records is encyclopaedic, and his memory of a long-ago conversation sets Matthias on the track of the sword itself, stolen from its secret resting place seasons before. When he falls to a foul blow from a renegade fox, his comrades mourn the passing of the gentlest mouse they have ever known.

## MATTHIAS

Appears in: *Redwall, Mattimeo*

From the moment Methuselah confirms that Martin the Warrior has foreseen the coming of Matthias, it is clear that there is something special about the clumsy young novice who has been admitted to the abbey as an orphaned woodland mouse. He gives an instinctive warrior's response to the threatened arrival of Cluny the Scourge: 'We'll be ready,' he says, and they are. Abbot Mortimer, as he lies dying, decrees that Matthias should not be Brother but Warrior and Champion of Redwall. As such he leads the expedition to rescue their kidnapped young ones; as such he returns victorious, and passes many seasons before handing on his sword and title. But, Warrior or not, he always helps to land the biggest fish for the seasonal feast!

## CORNFLOWER

Appears in: *Redwall, Mattimeo*

The quiet young fieldmouse is the prettiest creature Matthias has ever seen, and when the coming of Cluny the Scourge forces her family to take refuge in Redwall Abbey he is not altogether sorry. Their friendship is sealed when she comes across him weeping beneath the tapestry of Martin the Warrior, and, instead of despising him as he fears, encourages him with such loving understanding that Matthias is inspired. She is calm, practical and efficient, and quick-thinking in a crisis: the ideal mate for a warrior. And seasons later, when their son is kidnapped and Matthias goes in search of him, she plays a major role in the defence of the abbey, always thinking of others before herself.

## MATTIMEO

Appears in: *Mattimeo*

Matthias Methuselah Mortimer, Mattimeo for short, is Matthias and Cornflower's son, and a spoilt brat. But his one ambition is to wield the great sword of the warriors of Redwall Abbey, and it is his determination to earn this privilege that finally teaches him the value of obedience. When Slagar the Cruel descends on the abbey with his band of slavers, and steals the young ones away in the night, Mattimeo has to grow up very quickly indeed. By the time the captured youngsters have reached their destination, he is beginning to show true leadership, and when the opportunity arises to join their rescuers in the final underground battle he leads his friends into combat with all the courage of a seasoned warrior.

## SISTER ALKANET

Appears in: *The Taggerung*

The infirmary sister, though kind and considerate in the sickroom, is not a mouse to stand any nonsense in the general way of things – known for her icy glare, only very occasionally does she allow her deadpan sense of humour to peep through her stern exterior. Not above smacking a cheeky hare in the nose with a pudding spoon, she always makes her feelings plain, and hers is the only dissenting voice when Badgermum Cregga suggests that the ottermaid Mhera should take charge of the abbey defences when vermin are in the vicinity. Alkanet thinks Mhera is too young for the responsibility, and says as much, so it takes real heroism to admit, later, that it has been the right choice: that Mhera is truly the Mother Abbess of Redwall.

## NIMBALO THE SLAYER

Appears in: *The Taggerung*

Ill-treated by a brutal father until he is old enough to fight back, Nimbalo wants nothing to do with families or tribes, although friends are another matter: 'No mate o' mine fights standin' alone,' he tells Deyna. The otter Taggerung understands that much of Nimbalo's bravado can be laid at the door of his upbringing, and stands by like a true comrade while the harvest mouse makes his peace with the past. By the time their travels bring them to Redwall, Nimbalo can even enjoy the communal life of the abbey. Seeing him in his element, surrounded by good food and attentive company, surely nobeast can fail to be reminded of that other great teller of tales and singer of songs – Gonff the Mousethief!

## MARTIN THE WARRIOR

Appears in: *Martin the Warrior, Mossflower, The Legend of Luke*

The mousebabe is only a few days old when Vilu Daskar launches his murderous attack. The slaughter is terrible: the babe's mother is among the dead, and Martin himself only survives because his grandmother Windred falls as she is carrying him away and lies, covered with sand, while the killing goes on around them. When Martin's father returns, with the others of his foraging party, the camp is in ruins and Vilu gone. But Luke never forgets, and seasons later, on a captured ship, he sails away in search of the murderers. Before he leaves, he gives his sword to young Martin, telling him to use it well. And Martin does – until the day he is taken captive by Badrang the stoat, who steals the sword and enslaves the strong young mouse.

It is in Badrang's fortress that he first encounters Rose, his soul mate, and to Badrang that he  loses her, killed in the battle that is to see the tyrant's death at Martin's paws. From that moment on, though he has the best of friends in Gonff and Timballisto, Martin remains at heart aloof and alone. Unbeatable because invulnerable, he leads the woodlanders to victory against the wildcat Tsarmina; then, when he returns from the quest to find his father, he hangs up his sword and follows the way of peace.

He is Redwall Abbey's co-founder, its first Warrior and Champion, and its guiding spirit even after his death.

# Mice Mayhem ❖ ——

## HIDDEN GREATS

Mice make excellent scholars and are great at wordplay and riddles. Can you work out the names of these mice below?

1. Lambino
2. Nimble Ocu
3. Wolf Rocner
4. Hestemulah
5. Lemiar

6. Stamitah
7. Tammetio
8. Magerine
9. Dinnad
10. Stallimbito

## MARVELLOUS MICE

The mice of Redwall have many skills, whether in the field of battle, the kitchen or as healers. Can you match each mouse from the list on the left with the object that best matches their character on the right?

Rose
Mariel
Sister Alkanet
Cornflower
John Churchmouse
Gonff
Martin
Timballisto
Abbess Germaine

sword
healing herbs
ballista
flute
sheet of music
quill pen
cakes and ale
building plans
gullwhacker

## PRECOCIOUS PRINCE

Cheeky mouse Gonff considers himself the prince of many things but which of these titles does he not use to describe himself?

1. Prince of Mousethieves
2. Prince of Dancers
3. Prince of Escapers
4. Prince of Shanties

5. Prince of Climbers
6. Prince of Predictors
7. Prince of Toadwhackers
8. Prince of Players

# The Mice Quiz ❖ — ❖

1. What do Mattimeo and Tess name their son?

2. Which badgermaid discovers Martin's sword in the mouth of the Deepcoiler?

3. Which mouse is known as 'The Slayer'?

4. What is the name of the rat ship from which Martin rescues his old friend, Timballisto?

5. Which of the seven stone steps between the Great Hall and the Cavern Hole in the abbey hides the entrance to the tomb of Martin the Warrior?

6. What does Cornflower give Matthias to wear before he helps to defend the abbey?

7. What ingredient does Columbine add to her scone mix to turn it the colour of the abbey walls?

8. What is Rose's brother called?

9. For what is Guff the dormouse famed?

10. From where did the sparrows steal Martin's sword?

11. What type of bird that 'only flies one way' does Mariel find at the bottom of the rock pool?

12. What is the name of Rose's mother?

13. How do most of the Loamhedge mice help out at the battle of Kotir?

14. What device does Abbess Germaine use to help her hearing?

15. Which mouse deduces that Cluny is about to launch an attack from the elm tree?

16. What type of cake does Polleekin the molewife bake for Rose, Martin, Grumm the mole and Pallum the hedgehog?

17. After Methuselah, who is the only creature in Redwall able to read Loamscript?

18. Who provides the voice for the 'ghost' of Martin the Warrior?

19. Which small hedgehog tries to steal a knapsack from Mariel and Dandin?

20. What is Mattimeo's full name?

21. What gift does Aubretia the mousemaid present to Redwall after telling the story of Martin and Rose?